# The Secret Life of Fairies

WRITTEN BY

## Penelope Larkspur

ILLUSTRATED BY

## Leslie Elizabeth Watts

KIDS CAN PRESS

*For Colleen Margaret Wyatt — PL*

*For Emily and Stefan — LEW*

Kids Can Press acknowledges the financial support of the
Ontario Arts Council, the Canada Council for the Arts and
the Department of Cultural Heritage.

Published in Canada by      Published in the U.S. by
Kids Can Press Ltd.         Kids Can Press Ltd.
29 Birch Avenue             85 River Rock Drive, Suite 202
Toronto, ON  M4V 1E2        Buffalo, NY  14207

Edited by Charis Wahl
Designed by Marie Bartholomew
Printed and bound in Hong Kong by Book Art Inc., Toronto

CM 99  0 9 8 7 6 5 4 3 2 1

**Canadian Cataloguing in Publication Data**

Larkspur, Penelope
        The secret life of fairies

ISBN 1-55074-547-6
ISBN 1-55074-555-7 (book & necklace)

I. Watts, Leslie Elizabeth, 1961-    . II. Title.

PS8573.A678S42    1999      jC813'.54      C99-930313-9
PZ7.L32317Se    1999

Kids Can Press is a Nelvana company.

# Contents

❧

## Entering the Fairy World

Next time you are in the woods on a moonlit night, be on the lookout for fairies.

You may hear them before you see them. The thrum of a harp or the lilting melody of a flute will tell you they are nearby.

Approach quietly, for fairies do not like to be watched. If you are lucky, you may glimpse a troop of fairies dancing.

By the moon we sport and play,

Merry as the month of May.

As we dance, the dew doth fall;

Trip it, little urchins all,

Lightly as the little bee,

Two by two and three by three.

# A Fairy

This is a trooping fairy, so called because she belongs to a fairy troop. She is 211 years old. (Most fairies live for more than a thousand years so, in fairy terms, she is still very young.) She is practicing landing on a lily. The trick is to touch down without getting pollen smudges on your clothes.

Bees and fairies do not get along because they compete for the same food — nectar from flowers.

Hedgehog quills serve as arrows. Luckily for mice and other prey, fairies are not very good shots.

Magic wand

Most trooping fairies are fair haired.

Pollen smudge

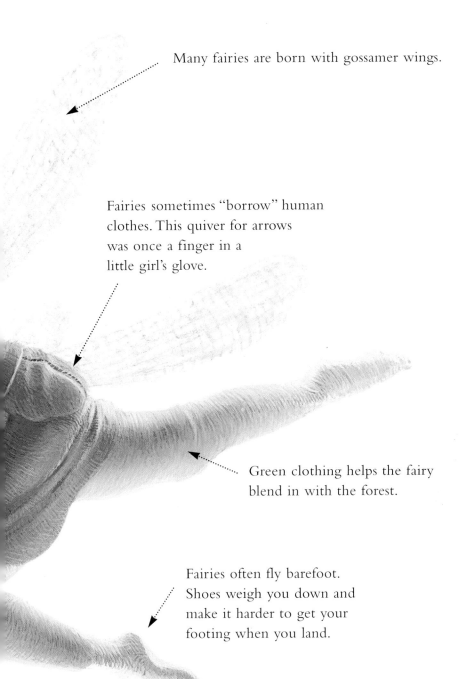

Many fairies are born with gossamer wings.

Fairies sometimes "borrow" human clothes. This quiver for arrows was once a finger in a little girl's glove.

Green clothing helps the fairy blend in with the forest.

Fairies often fly barefoot. Shoes weigh you down and make it harder to get your footing when you land.

Fairies do not have belly buttons.

Some common fairy names are Mab, Pinch, Puck, Sib and Puddlefoot. Other fairy names include Patch, Dryp, Licke, Gull and Terrytop.

## HOUSE FAIRIES

House fairies, sometimes called solitaries or brownies, are a very different kettle of fish. They are much bigger than trooping fairies. If one stood next to you, he would be up to your knees. Their red or brown clothes are often ragged. Most could use a good shampoo and haircut. It is said that house fairies are responsible for a lot of the mysterious things — good and bad—that happen around the house.

# Fairy Powers

Fairies are born with magical powers. Even fairy babies can make magic, although sometimes their spells go awry. A cranky baby may accidentally make its mother disappear. Two quarreling toddlers may turn each other into pigs and not know how to unpig themselves.

But as they grow up, fairies learn to use their four magical powers wisely.

## FLYING

Flying is one of a fairy's greatest joys. What better way to see the countryside! Some fairies have wings and can hover and dart like hummingbirds. Wingless fairies grab twigs (ragwort stems are a favorite) or tie some grass together and climb on. Then all it takes is a secret password. If you want to try it yourself, call out the magic words "horse and hattock" when you're ready to take off. Some fairies believe that wearing a white hat helps.

Fairies can also make humans fly through the air. One poor man accidentally fell asleep in a fairy forest and was sent flying. When he woke up, he was far away on a busy city street. His coat was gone, and his blue hat was dangling from a church steeple.

## TRANSFORMING

Fairies can make themselves bigger or smaller or turn themselves and others into animals. They call this "shape shifting." Cats are a popular shape to shift into. If you see a cat behaving oddly, it may be a fairy transformed.

Some people say that a fairy grows smaller with each transformation. This explains reports of fairies so small that they ride ants like horses.

## BECOMING INVISIBLE

When fairies want to escape danger — or make mischief — they can become invisible. People who have walked through an invisible fairy troop say they can sense the fairies all around them, jostling and whispering, but there is nothing to see. Becoming invisible takes a lot of energy, so fairies save it for important times.

Glamour is what fairies use to make you see what they want you to see. For instance, a fairy living in a rundown shed might use glamour to fool you into thinking it is a castle. Ugly fairies often use glamour to make themselves appear beautiful.

There is a way to see through glamour — wipe fairy ointment over your eyes. Fairy ointment is a mixture of four-leaf clovers and other magical ingredients, and it lets you see things as they really are, not as the fairies want you to see them.

## THE WAND

A wand is a fairy's prize possession. To operate a wand, you wave it back and forth through the air. As you wave, you cast a spell and point at the subject of your spell.

Long ago, fairies didn't use wands. They simply cast a spell. Usually that worked fine, but sometimes a magic spell got blown about by the wind, which could be dangerous. Instead of turning a bee into a butterfly, a fairy might accidentally turn it into a bull. Then, several hundred years ago, some wise fairy invented the wand. It channeled the magic and cut down on mishaps.

Besides spells and wishes, a magic wand can sprinkle fairy dust, which can make people sleep for a hundred years, suddenly become beautiful or ugly, and even fall in love with their enemies.

# Fairy Homes

Some fairies live in Fairyland. Others live by the hearth of human houses. But most live in fairy mounds in the woods.

From the outside, a fairy mound looks like a pile of earth overgrown with weeds. You have to search carefully to find the entrance, usually a small door near the base of a tree or inside a hollow log. Open the door gently and you might hear singing or smell cakes baking. If you could pass through it, here is what you would see.

Door

Fairies cook meals together in the kitchen. They take turns peeling vegetables and baking cakes and bread.

As in many human houses, the basement is a mess. It is stuffed to overflowing with things the fairies have dragged home.

Fairies like their privacy — especially
in the bathroom. No one has ever
seen inside a fairy bathroom.

Twigs are bent and nailed to make
furniture for the living room.
Sometimes a chair or sofa sprouts
leaves and turns into an indoor tree.

All the fairies eat together in one big
dining room. They use leaves for plates
and acorns for goblets. These dishes are
thrown out after every meal, so there
are never many dishes to wash.

Spiderwebs are dyed
and braided into cozy rugs.

To see a fairy bedroom, turn the page ...

# Inside a Fairy's Bedroom

Because fairy mounds are a bit cramped, fairies often have to share a bedroom. Fairies sometimes furnish their rooms with things that humans have lost or thrown away.

To prevent sleepflying, beds have canopies and curtains. If you have lost a roll of candies, a barrette or a pencil lately, look no farther.

Fireflies provide light. At night their cages are draped with a cloth so the light doesn't keep the fairies awake.

An empty matchbox makes a perfect bed, especially with a small sock for a sleeping bag. A tea bag makes a fragrant pillow.

No one, least of all fairies, likes stepping on a cold floor in the morning. A mouse hide next to the bed solves that problem.

Fairies like to have a goblet of water beside their bed at night so they don't have to walk to the bathroom in the dark if they get thirsty.

Wand holders

A silver spoon makes a good mirror.

The fireplace keeps things cozy in winter. A few wooden matches make a blaze that lasts for hours.

Books include such fairy favorites as *Peter Pan* and *The Lord of the Rings.*

Young fairies are gently tied in to stop them from flying in their sleep and getting lost in the dark.

# Fairy Fashions

Fairies are fussy about what they wear. They do not like clothes that pinch, rub or itch. And because they fly, their clothing must be lightweight, the lighter the better. Besides everyday green wear, most fairies have a wardrobe full of clothes for special occasions.

This delicate dress for a fancy-ball was spun from dew-draped spiderwebs. See how the dew-drops sparkle like diamonds?

A flower hat protects against rain or sun. Red or pink flowers are favorites, especially fuchsias and foxgloves. On windy days a fairy may clamp on a snapdragon.

When dancing or hunting, fairies insist on comfortable shoes. Mouse-skin shoes are as soft as velvet. Some vain fairies dye their shoes lemon yellow.

On wet fall nights, a fairy might put on a cape made out of bat wings. It sheds raindrops better than an umbrella.

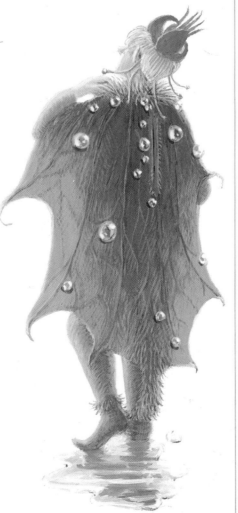

A knit hat lost in the woods can become cozy sweaters for a dozen fairies.

# Fairy Food

There is nothing fairies like better than a feast. Butter, milk, cream and cheese are their favorite foods. While some fairies make their own dairy products, many prefer to steal from humans. If you run out of milk or find the butter missing from your sandwich, the fairies may be to blame.

Some people say that fairies do not actually steal food — they just take the essence or "foyson" and leave the rest behind. A tasteless bit of cheese may have been delicious before the fairies got to it.

Bread is an important fairy food. (You can sometimes attract fairies by leaving out a nice thick slab of buttered bread.) Many fairies bake their own bread. They slice the loaves right out of the oven and eat them warm with butter.

Fairies also harvest food that grows in the wild. Bluebells are a favorite. Fairies eat them steamed, creamed or boiled. Eating blue food doesn't seem to bother them.

Here is a typical day's menu for a fairy.

### BREAKFAST

*Seed porridge with dried berries*

*Cream sweetened with nectar*

*A bowl of milk*

### LUNCH

*A gooseberry sandwich with lots of butter*

*A bowl of milk*

### DINNER

*Cream of bluebell soup*

*A nut burger with essence of cheese*

*on a buttered bun*

*Dandelion-leaf salad*

*Fairy cakes with cream icing (see recipe)*

*A bowl of milk*

### BEDTIME SNACK

*A bowl of warm milk with a pat of butter*

*Leftover fairy cakes (if available)*

### FAIRY CAKES WITH CREAM ICING

Actual fairy cakes are about the size of raspberries. Since it is hard to find baking pans that small, you can bake them in a muffin tin.

#### INGREDIENTS

| | | |
|---|---|---|
| 500 mL | flour | 2 c. |
| 10 mL | baking powder | 2 tsp. |
| 5 mL | salt | 1 tsp. |
| 175 mL | butter | 3/4 c. |
| 375 mL | white sugar | 1 1/2 c. |
| 3 | eggs | 3 |
| 5 mL | vanilla | 1 tsp. |
| 325 mL | milk | 1 1/3 c. |

1. Grease the muffin tin with a bit of butter.

2. Sift together the flour, baking powder and salt.

3. Cream together the butter and sugar, then add the eggs and vanilla. Beat until light and fluffy.

4. Add a few spoonfuls of dry ingredients then some milk to the creamed mixture. Keep alternating ingredients until well mixed.

5. Fill the muffin cups three-quarters full. Bake at 180°C (350°F) for 20 to 25 minutes.

6. Let cool before frosting with your favorite icing.

# Fairy Life

If the fairies had their way, they would dance and feast all day.

But even fairies have chores ...

This hunting party hopes to bag a mouse. The dogs are working animals, not pets.

The king and queen of the troop supervise and settle arguments.

Taking care of trees, especially oak and elder, is a serious responsibility. A human who tries to cut down a tree under the fairies' protection may find that his luck suddenly turns bad.

Fairies gather plants with special healing powers. Forget-me-nots improve the memory. Sneezewort cures sniffles. And a tonic made from speedwell cheers up fairies who are feeling blue. A fairy who drinks too much of it may become tipsy.

The milk from fairy cows makes
the dairy products fairies love.

Fairy horses are used for hunting
and for processions called "rades."
They are kept gleaming white.

To relax, fairies play chess or
practice hurling, a sport
similar to field hockey.

Fairies are skilled spinners and weavers.
They do lovely embroidery with spider
silk dyed a rainbow of colors.

# Fairy Watching

How can you see fairies? Here is some advice from Lewis Carroll, author of *Alice's Adventures in Wonderland*:

*The first rule is, that it must be a very hot day — that we may consider settled: and you must be just a little sleepy — but not too sleepy to keep your eyes open, mind. Well, and you ought to feel a little — what one may call "fairyish" — the Scotch call it "eerie," and perhaps that's a prettier word; if you don't know what it means, I'm afraid I can hardly explain it; you must wait until you meet a Fairy, and then you'll know.*

*And the last rule is, that the crickets should not be chirping …*

*So, if all things happen together, you have a good chance of seeing a Fairy …*

Here are more tips on fairy watching from people who have seen them.

The best times for seeing fairies are twilight, midnight, noon and the hour before dawn. These are the most magical times of day. Most fairy sightings happen in midsummer.

Peer through a stone that has a hole worn through it by wind or waves. These are called "self-bored stones" and are thought to be a window into the fairy world.

Look for a circle in the dirt or grass. It could be a fairy ring worn bare by tiny dancing feet. Hide behind a bush and wait — the fairies may return to dance some more.

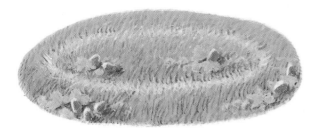

Put a four-leaf clover on your head and hold it in place with a hat or scarf. One young girl who put a clump of grass and clover on her head to cushion a milk pail suddenly saw that she was surrounded by fairies.

Be careful to stay out of sight. If the fairies catch you watching them, they may pinch you black and blue or tie you up with spiderwebs.

## ATTRACTING FAIRIES TO YOUR GARDEN

Over the years people have found ways to attract fairies to gardens. In fact some fairies now live permanently at the bottom of gardens. Here are some do's and don'ts to attract fairies.

Do plant bluebells, a traditional fairy food, and red or pink flowers that are suitable for hats.

Don't plant Saint John's wort — fairies hate it and will stay away from any garden that has it.

Do leave out a dish of milk. Fairies like to wash their babies in a milk bath.

Don't leave out a horseshoe or other iron object. There was never a fairy born who liked iron. No one knows why.

# Fairies and People

Suppose you were lucky enough to befriend some trooping fairies or discover a brownie living in your house. What should you expect? Fairies have rules about how people (and fairies) should behave. Follow their rules and things will go smoothly. Break them at your peril.

## RULE 1

Never ever call them "fairies." For some reason, they consider this an invasion of privacy and will instantly disappear. Or pinch you as punishment. Instead, call them the Good People, the Gentle Folk, the Gentry, the Wee Folk or the People of Peace.

## RULE 2

Keep things tidy. Nothing bothers a fairy more than a mess. A house fairy will whirl around cleaning up, and then expect you to keep things neat. But fairies can be touchy. A woman who kept her house too clean came home one day to find food spilled, furniture upended, and ashes scattered everywhere.

## RULE 3

Do not insult fairies by overpaying for tasks they do for you. When a farmer left a new set clothes for a ragged fairy who had threshed his grain, the fairy was offended. He scattered grain everywhere and was never seen again. A slice of bread with lots of butter and a dish of milk is all the payment fairies want.

### RULE 4

Be polite and courteous. Fairies do not take kindly to those who are rude. Courtesy is rewarded. A man once courteously agreed to move a drain so that water didn't flood the home of a fairy living under his house. Many years later, the man was about to be executed when the fairy rode up on a white horse and rescued him.

### RULE 5

If the fairies take something from you, do not try to get it back. Fairies take only what people do not take care of or refuse to share. When a farmer stopped the fairies from taking milk from one of her cows, they got even by turning the cow's milk sour.

### RULE 6

Never steal from fairies. A man who took a golden cup from a fairy woke the next morning to find that one of his legs had gone lame. And the cup was gone. In its place was an ugly toadstool.

# Fairy Relatives

Fairies have hundreds of relatives, some close, some more distant, in all parts of the world. There are boggy-boes, hobthrusts, pad-fooits, tutgots, boggarts, gallytrots, miffies, lubberkins, clabbernappers, thrummy-caps, puckles, tod-lowries and many more. Here are some well-known fairy "cousins."

## FAIRY GODMOTHERS

Cinderella had one. Everyone needs one. Fairy godmothers, who first appeared in France, can turn the ordinary into the beautiful. A pumpkin becomes a carriage, rags become a glorious ball gown — all with the wave of a wand. Fairy godmothers are the special protectors of children. Should you get into trouble, call on them by name. Three names to try are Arcile, Morgue and Maglore.

## ELVES

If you had a penny for every elf on Earth, you would be rich. Most elves are a lot like trooping fairies, except they live in Elfame, not Fairyland. Some live at the North Pole and work for Santa Claus. Others live underground and can be wicked. An injury caused by one of their flint-tipped arrows (elf-shot) can cause a bad wound or sickness, so it's best to stay clear of them.

## LEPRECHAUNS

These Irish spirits are shoe-makers of great skill. They earn huge sums of money from their work and hide their gold in big black pots in caves or at the end of a rainbow. If you see a leprechaun, do not take your eyes off him for a moment. While he is in your sight, he is under your power and may lead you to his treasure. But look away for an instant and — *pffft!* — he will be gone.

### GOBLINS

These mischievous or wicked fairy relatives can be a real nuisance around the house. They turn food bad, knock dishes off shelves, and generally make a terrible mess. Fortunately they prefer to live in cold, wet places, not houses.

Add "hob" to "goblin" and you get a hobgoblin, a spirit that is more mischief than malice. Hobgoblins also go by the name of spriggans, bugbears and redcaps.

### DOMOVOI

Close relatives of brownies (see page 7), domovoi are the hairiest of the fairy folk. They live in Russian homes, often beside the stove. While they moan and groan a fair amount, they are basically kindly and will alert a family to fire or other house dangers. Sometimes they seem to like the house better than the people. When a family moves, the domovoi may have to be bribed to go along.

### PIXIES

Pixies ride around on ponies about the size of dogs. A warning: if you come across one, do not ask for directions. Pixies are famous for getting people lost. There is even a name for it: pixie-led. There have also been reports of some pixies stealing children and using magic ointment to keep them from growing. Fortunately most are friendly and helpful — except when it comes to giving directions.

# A Fairy Tale

Anna and Marion sat on a hard bench, picking dirt and twigs out of a basket of wool. There was no fire to warm them, and their fingers were stiff with cold. Beside them in a cradle, their baby brother, Tom, whimpered.

"Poor babe. He's hungry," said Anna.

"Aye," nodded Marion. But there was nothing they could do for him.

As the last of the wool was cleaned, the front door flew open. A huge man carried another basket piled with dirty wool. "Clean this, you two, and more to come." He threw down the basket. "I'll teach you to take cake of mine."

"But, Stepfather, we were hungry," said Marion.

"You'll eat what I give you — when I give it. Now get back to work."

That night the two girls lay in their tiny bed, shivering and hungry. "If only Mother were alive," said Anna. Her eyes filled with tears.

"Think of Mother's shortcake with berries," said Marion to cheer her, but that only made them sadder and hungrier.

"I know!" said Marion, sitting bolt upright in bed. "Potatoes. There must be some potatoes left in the field." She took the ragged blanket from their bed and wrapped it over the sleeping Tom. Anna bent to kiss him. Then, quiet as mice, they crept out the door and into the potato field.

The moon was a crescent in the sky. The trees were almost bare. The night air whispered winter. In the field they dug and dug, unearthing the last potatoes.

When they had as many as they could carry in their outstretched nightgowns, they headed home. They crossed grass crisp with frost. Suddenly, a gleam of light shone from behind an oak tree. Anna put her hand on Marion's arm. "What was that?" They stood stark still.

The light glimmered again, and they could hear the faint sound of flutes and singing voices. Marion put her finger to her lips. Together they crept toward the oak, bent so low they were almost crawling, leaving a trail in the frost.

Marion took a deep breath and peered around the oak. There, in a clearing, was a procession of fairies mounted on white horses not much bigger than mice. Moonlight glinted off the gold and jewels that draped both riders and mounts. "Look, Anna," Marion whispered. "A fairy rade!"

But quiet as she was, the fairies heard her. Their horses twisted and snorted in surprise. The fairy archers pointed tiny golden bows in her direction. One false move and they would let their arrows fly.

Marion slowly stood. "We mean you no harm," she said quietly, to calm them. Anna rose beside her, and the two girls huddled together for comfort.

The horses' bridles jingled, and wind poured through whistles hung from their manes. The finest of all the riders led the procession. Jewels glinted like stars on her white robe. Gold chains and green scarves twined around her neck, and she wore a crown no bigger than a finger ring.

"I am queen of these people," she said. "And you are mere mortals, not worthy to see a rade." The girls tried to speak, but she put up one tiny hand. She looked at the potatoes and saw how thin the girls were. Her face softened. "No mind," she said. "You're poor hungry mortals. You shall come to our home."

"We cannot leave our brother, m'am. He's —" Marion began, but the Fairy Queen waved her wand and all sight and sound faded.

When the girls awoke, the air was as warm as a midsummer's day and filled with the perfume of cinnamon and cloves. Over them was a quilt as light as a feather with a covering of the richest silk.

"Wh-where are we?" asked Anna, her voice filled with wonder.

Outside, golden light filtered through trees filled with fruit. One gleaming perfect pear was just within the girls' reach. Through the trees a stream burbled, and red and white cattle grazed nearby. A swallow darted past with two tiny children on its back. Marion's eyes widened.

"Are we in heaven?" asked Anna.

"No. This must be Fairyland."

Anna reached for the pear, but Marion pulled her hand back. "Anna, no! Remember the stories? If you eat their food, you can never return home."

"Why should we go home?" asked Anna, struggling to free her hand. "It is warm as summer here, and there is food."

"And what about poor wee Tom?"

There was a soft knock at the door, and a

group of fairies entered the room carrying a platter of cheeses and fruits and bread so fragrant the girls could taste it. Although the fairies' food was tempting, nothing could persuade Anna and Marion to eat it. Not then, nor any time for the next seven days. Instead they ate their mortal food — cold rough potatoes from the field.

On the seventh day, the Fairy Queen came to see them. She pointed to the perfect pear outside their window. "Eat and you will be one of us and spend your days dancing and singing."

Marion shook her head. "We must go home, m'am. Our young brother needs us."

"Ah," said the Fairy Queen. "Then take the pear with you. If ever you wish to return to this place, take one bite each."

No sooner were the words spoken than the room and the silken bed and the Fairy Queen were gone. In their place, strange carriages with no horses sped past, forcing the girls to jump out of the way. A forest of houses stretched so tall that the girls could not see the tops. Bright lights blinked in their eyes.

"We are free from Fairyland," said Anna, clinging to Marion, "but what is this strange place?" A sign by the side of the road answered her question. It was their village, but so changed they could not recognize it.

Marion grabbed Anna's hand. "Come. We must find Tom."

All day they looked, but nothing was familiar. As they wandered, children jeered and pointed at their clothing. Harsh music seemed to play itself, and the air was thick with smells that made them cough. Finally, at dusk, Anna spied a gnarled old oak. Though bent and twisted, it reminded them of the tree they had

left just seven days earlier. The house behind it was falling down with neglect, but a light burned in the window. Marion opened a rickety gate and they walked up the path and knocked on the door.

Inside there was shuffling, then slowly the door creaked open. Leaning on it was a man as old and bent as the oak and as broken down as the house.

"Sir, please," said Anna. "We are searching for our brother. His name is Tom Wyatt."

The old man looked away, as if peering back through time. His voice was the rasping whisper of one who seldom talks. "My name is Tom Wyatt," he said, "but you cannot be my sisters. They disappeared one wintry night nigh eighty years ago."

Anna looked at the old man, then at the house and tree. "Oh, what have the fairies done!" she shrieked. "One week in Fairyland, and eighty years have passed."

Anna reached into her pocket and pulled out the pear. "Sir, take one bite of this pear and you will see your sisters again."

The old man's pale blue eyes looked deeply into hers. He reached out for the pear and took a bite. Then Anna and Marion bit into the pear. Suddenly, the air was as warm as a midsummer's day and scented with cinnamon and cloves.

From a tower high up in her castle, the Fairy Queen smiled. Through the shimmering light at the edge of the forest, two girls and their baby brother were coming home.

# Farewell to the Fairies

No one knows where fairies came from. Some think they are a race of small people chased off into the woods by conquerors. There they became smaller and smaller and gained their magical powers. Other people believe that fairies are fallen angels.

One thing is sure. Fairies are slowly disappearing. It's not difficult to see why. The forests where they live are being cut down. The meadows where they gather food are being plowed under. And not many houses have a hearth that a fairy can call home.

But do not lose heart. There are fairies all over the world, and there are sure to be some where you live. Go out on a midsummer's eve, just as the sky is darkening. Be very still and listen for the sounds of voices singing and a harp thrumming. Then, ever so quietly, move closer for a good look.

# Fairy-sighting Form

| Date | Time of day | Description of fairies | Notes |
|------|-------------|------------------------|-------|
|      |             |                        |       |
|      |             |                        |       |
|      |             |                        |       |
|      |             |                        |       |